The Pushover Plot

A Stella Madison Caper

Lilly Maytree

Lightsmith Publishers
Thorne Bay, Alaska

ISBN: 978-1-944798-47-5

Published in the United States by

Lightsmith Publishers
P.O. Box 19293
Thorne Bay, Alaska 99919

Website: www.LightsmithPublishers.com

Cover photography by Steve and Becky Brown

Lightsmith Publishers is an imprint of the Wilderness School Institute, a non-profit educational organization that offers outdoor youth activities in wilderness settings, including training in wilderness skills and nature studies, as well as the publication of curriculum on related subjects, through the Wilderness School Press, and their children's imprint Summers Island Press.

The Pushover Plot / Paperback Edition

*To those who have had to contend with
the darker side of supernatural—
may you never be left there.*

"A lie that is half-truth is the darkest of all lies."

Alfred Tennyson

1

Stella Madison walked down the long dark hallway and deliberately ignored the flutter of fear it gave her. It was ridiculous, really, considering how many others were nearby who wouldn't hesitate to respond to any call for help. Then a regular jolt replaced that flutter because she suddenly remembered how often her own fears had robbed her of her voice in the most desperate hours. Something which made her revert to the old childhood trick of darting from safety to safety as fast as she possibly could.

So, having left the warm comfort at the side of her sleeping husband, she veered toward what had originally been known as the First Mate's cabin, to listen for the deep, reassuring snores of Mason Jeffries. Then to the faint sliver of light shining beneath Gerald's door (who still slept with a light on to "orient himself" even though they had all been aboard the *Dreadnaught* for nearly a month). After that, it was only a hop and a skip to the galley, where Millie left a light on over the stove in case anyone should get hungry in the middle of the night and come looking for a snack.

In fact, she began to hear somebody moving around in there as she got closer, along with the distinctly delicious smell of Ovaltine (why, she hadn't tasted any of that in years!). Evidence that someone beside herself hadn't been able to sleep, either. How nice it would be to enjoy a quiet chat instead of wading through the predawn hour all alone. Millie needing to take one of her pills, maybe, or Lou, up with the baby for some reason. Although if it was Captain Stuart, she probably wouldn't stay long as he was about the oddest person she had ever known. Not counting mentally deranged people which she had seen more than her share of.

Funny how memories from so long ago came suddenly to mind at certain times.

"I guess I'm not the only one who couldn't sleep," she spoke quietly as she pushed through the door, so as not to startle whoever it was. Only no one answered. Instead, she caught just a glimpse of someone disappearing through the companionway door on the far side of the sailboat's galley that led down to below decks. Someone in a full-length, light-colored gown and a dark braid that hung halfway down their back.

Stella got goosebumps when she saw that because none of the Dreadnaught's crew had hair that long. She reached for the corner of the large iron stove to steady herself but got even more of a fright to discover it was stone cold. No one had been heating any hot chocolate in here. Maybe it had been another stowaway. Considering all the dark nooks and crannies in this vessel and how many weeks Lou Edna had managed to hide her young man without a one of them having the slightest idea... it was a possibility.

A better one than the alternative, anyway.

Besides, how could those terrible things be happening, again, when she was cured of all that so long ago? Especially when her wonderful new life had just begun. They couldn't be! There simply had to be another explanation. She pulled open the narrow cupboard next to the stove where they kept all the hot drink supplies, and began to rummage through. Teas, coffee, hot cider, bouillon, hot chocolate... but no Ovaltine. That distinct mixture of malt in it was unmistakable. A realization that turned the cozy galley intimidating and made her want nothing more than to hurry back to where she belonged.

Along with another urge to have that talk with the colonel about her not-so-ordinary past that she kept putting off. In a few quick steps she was pushing back through the door, again, but only to collide with what looked like an old woman wrapped in a shawl, fairly gliding down the shadowy companionway.

At the same time Stella toppled backward, a distinctly male voice hollered, "Away, you foul spirit!" before tripping right over the top of her and landing hard on the other side. Along with an empty mug and sauce pan that clattered across the floorboards. "What—what? Good grief! Stella! Is it really you?"

"Of course, it's me! That's an awful thing to call someone, Gerry."

"What are you—doing—wandering around this time of night in that—that whatever it is?"

"It's my white terry with a Chinese collar." She got to her feet, feeling rather silly now that someone else was there. "I'm not going to say what I thought you were, with that cut-in-half serape you always wear on top of everything."

"I detest being cold, and the rest got in the way of my arms." He took the hand she offered, to get himself up off the floor. "Sorry for the name-calling. But—blast!" It was part of a Captain Stuart phrase (after a month at sea, they were all talking like old salts), "You scared the daylights out of me! Took you for another one of those ghastly apparitions."

"You mean, you actually saw one?"

"One? They're all over the place around here. Getting so a man can't even hot up his Ovaltine without running into the things."

So, she did smell Ovaltine! Stella laughed out of sheer relief. "You don't know how glad I am to hear that. But the stove's cold, how did you do it?"

"Have a hotplate in my room but no sink. And I don't find anything in the least funny about it. All this rot, it's—it's serious business." He pushed the black watch-cap farther back on his head and then picked up his dishes. "Makes me rue the day I ever went gallivanting after such stuff. If I only knew then what I know now!"

"I'm sorry, Gerry. I wasn't making fun. I just had sort of a scare, myself. I'm glad it was you I ran into and not... something else."

"Yes, well... I must say, it's things like this that made it necessary to switch my major to botany from Medieval history, if you want to know the truth."

"I thought you told me your degree was in archeology." They went back through the cabinway door into the galley. "Even said you taught a few semesters of it at the junior level. Remember?"

"Yes, of course. It's how I originally landed a contract from the private school I worked at for so long. When a position opened up in the biology department, I jumped at the chance to get out of it and back into botany, again. Especially since I was working on my master's by the time."

"Oh. I thought you said you were working on a master's in archeology."

"I was, originally. However, it was worse than the Medieval, what with all those cursed artifacts we were forever digging up. Didn't like it at all after I'd finished. And the thought of spending so many hours in dusty museum basements, cleaning and cataloging them... well, they were as bad as the castles— worse even. Then, again, it might have just been me. Now, I actually think the things followed me over from England. That's where I first opened the door to them, anyway."

"The apparitions?"

"Seems like it. I tell you, that whole castle study was a nightmare. Never even finished out the class."

"I don't blame you. There's nothing worse than being scared out of your wits." Then she corrected herself. "Other than being dead, altogether."

"Sometimes I think I might as well be, the way it's ruined my life." He turned on the water at the sink in the far corner to rinse out his things, and the soft whir of the water pump went on. "Oh, and that bosh about them not being able to travel over water? Isn't true. Not one bit. It's been ten times worse since I came home."

"You mean, you're not Millie's cousin from England? Then why do you talk that way?" Stella was beginning to wonder if Gerald might be one of those compulsive liars, that you couldn't believe a word from. Or, a mentally unstable type that could have been helped in hospitals but never qualified for the programs because they weren't dangerous. The kind more easily controlled with medication. He did take an unbelievable amount of pills every day.

"Oh, we're cousins, all right. Born and raised in the same town. But it's a... well, it's a fake accent." He glanced over at her with a slight apologetic smile, just enough to show the space between his two front teeth. "Started when I went to college. You know, to impress people. Now, I can't quit."

"It's more old English than modern, you know. I keep expecting you to burst out with "forsooth!" or something."

"Or, dastardly," he added, "It's true, I do like the old phrases best. Always have. I like to think I was born out of time, except —with the high infant mortality back then—I probably wouldn't have made it past the age of three. Rate I'm going, now isn't much better, though. Putting up with all this when I'm hardly past fifty."

"You attribute some of your physical ailments to these...um... apparitions, too?"

"Mostly. The shaking, the weakness, insomnia... that sort of thing."

Stella gave a thoughtful sigh and sat down on the tufted burgundy cushions (that were a bit threadbare and oil-stained) surrounding the dining area. "I've been seeing an apparition, too, Gerry," she suddenly confessed. "I thought it was all in my mind.

Hallucinations, or something. But two people can't both be having the same hallucinations. Right?"

"Highly unlikely." He came over to sit across from her, still drying his hands on a blue dishtowel. "What have you been doing to get rid of yours? We should compare notes."

"I never knew you could get rid of them. I thought they just happened."

"Of course you can get rid of them. Or, so I've heard. There's a whole theological philosophy about that. Haven't had any luck with it, myself, yet, but I've only just started trying. Meanwhile, mind telling me how you cope?"

"Cope with what?"

"How you deal with it all. You know, the ugliness, the torment, and—"

"The what?"

"And the out-and-out filth!"

"Good heavens!" She shuddered at the very thought. "I haven't seen anything as terrible as all that! Only a lovely middle-aged woman from some bygone era. And only a couple of times."

"Then I must caution you to be careful," he warned. "They never stay lovely for long."

Stella woke up the next morning to the smell of freshly brewed coffee and the humming of the engine as it chugged along underneath them. By the way the sunlight was shining in through the porthole beside the bed, she could tell it had to be at least eight-o'clock, already. She had overslept. Either that or she was reluctant to leave the cozy comfort of her bed after a night like the last.

She was determined to have that talk with the colonel, sometime today. No matter what.

But not during his writing time. He put so much into his work she didn't have the heart to distract him with anything else before he finished his "daily stint." She had always been in awe of writers. How they could chronicle things in a way that made you feel you were actually living through the period, yourself; or even create another world, entirely. She fully believed reading good books had saved her from some of the darkest times in her life. It was also why she now had a collection of thousands.

"You're missing some beautiful scenery, dearest." The colonel popped in with his usual cheerfulness just long enough to set a steaming mug down on the built-in nightstand. "We even have fresh cinnamon rolls, this morning. Seems our Millie has been out-doing herself in the baking department, again."

"I think it takes her mind off leaving everything she's ever known and a kitchen is her most comfortable place." Stella sat up and plumped her pillow into a better position to lean against. "Thank you, dear. I'll be right out and we can enjoy the view together."

She threw on a pair of jeans and a navy knit sweater, then ran a quick brush through her hair. Knowing it would be a long trip she had it cut a bit shorter before she left. A month later and it seemed just right to turn under in the usual manner with her touch of natural curl.

Stella's hair had gone prematurely white (which she had several theories about). But thinking of it just now, she realized having white hair was the only thing that could have allowed her to do what she had been forced to do all those years, ago. So, looking at it in the perspective of her spiritual awakening, she could see how it had actually been providential.

That perhaps God had been looking after her even when she didn't know he was. What a comforting thought! If—in the times when she didn't know how to call out to him—he had dropped life-saving information and coincidences into her path in spite of herself.

Oliver already had their wooden tray set up in the middle of the couch (or settee, as it was called in nautical terms) when she joined him. That way, they could each sit at either end, and watch the beautiful scenery slip away behind them through the bank of French windows above it.

"Ready for a refill?" he asked, taking up the silver and glass French press they made coffee in every morning, here in their quarters. It had become customary for everyone to fend for themselves for breakfast and lunch to accommodate individual ship-board duties (as Captain Stuart called them). But they all gathered for family dinners each night.

"Just a warm-up," she replied. "I still

have half a cup. Didn't want to miss any of the show."

"And what a show it is, this morning. See how close we're traveling between these two rocky islands? Look how the water is so still our wake is nothing more than a wide ripple in the shape of a V spreading out behind us."

"It's the most beautiful place I've ever seen in my life."

"Absolutely magnificent!"

"And those tall sun-warmed pines—I could smell them wafting in through the open porthole. It was just glorious. Made me think back to summer camp days when I was growing up. Funny how things of nature impress you so much more in your youth."

The colonel glanced over at her with a mild surprise—he had one of the most expressive faces she had ever seen. Sometimes, she was sure she could tell exactly what he was feeling without him having to say a single word. Especially when he was working away at his writing. Now, a glint of delighted enthusiasm came into his gray eyes and she was sure he had hit on a break-through, or conquered some road-block in his current manuscript this morning.

"Interesting you should bring that up, Stel! Because I was having the very same thoughts, myself, this morning. Young people being so impressionable, and all."

"Isn't that amazing. Only married a month and already we're starting to think the same thoughts. What brought it on?" "A bit of inspiration that dropped into my mind and fit like a glove." He set his coffee down, put his hands on his knees with a decisive smack, and said, "My dear, I have decided to write a book for boys!"

Another coincidence! Wasn't she thinking about important information being "dropped down" at vital times only a few minutes ago? Oliver had called it an inspiration, and simply taken it in stride. If it truly was a piece of information from heaven—designed especially for them—what a wonderful way to live that would be! At least, that's how Stella was thinking about it just then.

"Are you talking about one of your hero books scaled down to a reading level for younger people? Why, Oliver, I think that would be marvelous." She cut a piece of cinnamon roll off with her fork and popped in in her mouth. "Mmm. Light, perfectly spiced, with just a touch of almond flavor in the glaze."

"I don't think they can get any closer to perfect."

"No doubt. But back to heroes. Your stories are so good. Even more so because they're true. I don't think children get enough truth these days. In fact none of us do. When I taught school it seemed like so much that was offered to young people was beneath them."

She paused for a moment, wondering, hit on a bit of logic that seemed to fit, then continued her thinking out loud. "I remember there was some new philosophy going around that students had short attention spans. But you know something? Maybe they were simply bored by things that really didn't have any depth. And, Oliver?"

"Yes, keep going—I like how our thoughts keep running in the same directions."

"Well, I think boys would find stories about heroes anything but boring. Or even too difficult. In fact, I believe they would rise to it."

"That's exactly it, Stell—they will rise to it! Only I'm not going to write them a story about heroes. I'm going to write one that will show them how to become one." Then he threw back his silver-haired head and laughed at the sheer pleasure of the thought. It was so delightful and catching Stella couldn't help laughing with him.

"And I know just how to do it, too!" he declared. "Because I know boys like the back of my own hand!"

At ten o'clock, Stella went into the galley to get a start on the lasagna she would be making for dinner. The place wasn't half as scary in the daytime. Especially with everyone coming through on various errands or simply to get a bit of something to nibble on. There was a large porthole over the sink where one could look out while chopping vegetables or doing dishes, and today it was so lovely it practically took her breath away.

They were moving through a place called Johnstone Strait, after some particularly tricky maneuvering through another place called the Seymour Narrows. They had to leave an hour earlier than the usual schedule in order to catch the narrows at slack tide. But Captain Stuart knew his stuff—he had even taken this route once before. Of course that was many years ago, and he had been driving a tugboat back then. Hauling shipping containers full of all manner of merchandise and personal effects bound for Alaska.

Now, the danger was past and the waterway had opened up into a long, wide channel of lovely pine-forested islands, with little coves and harbors to pull into. Should anyone take a fancy to do that. However, the crew of the *Dreadnaught* had fallen into the comfortable routine of setting out at seven each morning (if there wasn't a fog), and then being settled at anchor somewhere else between six or seven in the evening. Which was always daylight this time of year because the sun rose somewhere around five-thirty, and didn't disappear until after nine in these northern latitudes.

Stella was thinking about all these things when Cole DeForio (that handsome young man Lou Edna had smuggled aboard when they first left California, and had now become their much-appreciated First Mate) came in looking for Millie. It wasn't until she looked up from scattering freshly-grated Parmesan cheese over her second layer to tell him Millie was taking a nap, that she noticed he had the Senator tucked under one arm as if he were a football instead of a baby.

"Oh, good heavens, Cole..." She wiped her hands on her apron and reached for the toddler. "That's no way to--"

But the boy was having the time of his life (such a good- natured baby!) and gave her a big grin when she turned him right-side up, again.

"I don't know anything about babies," the young man replied. "Only bringing him to Lou or Millie so Gerald can take his turn at the wheel."

"Nonsense." Stella couldn't help reverting to her teacher- tone at such a remark. "I can tell you everything you need to know about them in two sentences. They're just little people. Give them the same respect you would anyone else and they'll love you forever."

"Kid doesn't even talk, Mrs. H, what's to respect?"

Cole had a beautiful smile to set off his dark hair and rugged handsomeness and he must have known it. Because Stella had never seen anyone who had so perfected the art of charming others. In spite of which she was completely taken in by him, herself. Then again, she had always had a soft spot for the restless types, especially when their hearts held the least bit of sensitivity toward others. Which this young man's did. Not to mention the unashamed gratefulness he carried for

Captain Stuart, who promoted him to First Mate status rather than sending him to jail.

"The same things you respect in any other person," she replied. "Like holding him right-side up, for starters. Then look him in the eye and call him by his name."

"Senator's no name for a regular person—especially a squirt like that." He reached a muscular forearm in front of her (that sported a tattoo of a ship's anchor), to snatch some of the Parmesan she had been grating. "I don't know what Lou was thinking to name him that. Isn't going to make things better for him, only worse."

"I'm inclined to agree with you but it wasn't our decision." "Do you call him Senny, or Torry? I don't like either." "Call him anything you want, as long as it's nice. That's what I do." Then, by way of demonstration, she held the child up until his darling little face was on a level with her her own, smiled her friendliest smile, and said, "Hi, Sonny Boy! Would you like a cracker?"

To which he gave a delighted squeal and **nearly bounced out of her arms in** anticipation.

Cole laughed at the obvious answer and ruffled the baby's dark curls. "OK. I get it. Mind keeping him a while? Lou and I had some... uh...words, last night. We need to talk."

"I'd be happy to. I'll put him in his high chair and give him a snack."

Which was exactly what Stella was busy doing when he was back not five minutes after he disappeared down the companionway steps, as if there was a fire in the engine room, or something.

"We gotta turn the boat around!" He was headed for the wheelhouse, on his way out the other door that led to the decks. "Lou's Gone!"

After that, a near panic ensued.

No one objected to turning around—of course they would turn around—but what had gotten into the girl? She left the ship without permission. Something that was a near sin, in Captain Stuart's estimation. Besides that, he informed them all, it was no small thing to turn around. This because they couldn't just chug back through Seymour Narrows without waiting for the tide to turn.

"Why can't we shove it full throttle and push right on through, Stuart?" Gerald had lost all color in his face at the news and was shaking with worry as he turned the wheel over to more capable hands. "Blast! It's an emergency!"

"Because of the blasted nineteen-knot current roaring through there about now, Gerald. We only do ten. When she's in top condition." The Captain checked fore and aft, to make sure there were no other nearby vessels, then gave the wheel an expert spin to start the turn.

He didn't look like a captain should, with that mop of gray hair sticking out in all directions, and those bushy black eyebrows that nearly made a strait line across his forehead when he squinted his eyes to look at something. And he didn't dress like one, either. But Stella had to admit his threadbare (oversized) black sweater, faded jeans, and tennis shoes with no socks, did not seem to effect his expertise in handling his own boat.

"Oh, that girl's going to be the death of me!" Millie sank down onto one of two deck chairs that were at either end of the wheelhouse. The left side of her auburn twist was falling out of the hair-clip, since she had been roused from her nap.

All seven of them were crowded into the small enclosure, not counting the Senator, who was seated comfortably on Stella's hip, avidly watching the drama unfold, and mirroring each speaker's expression as they spoke.

"It's not like Shortcake to up and leave without saying anything." Mason pushed his fisherman's cap farther back on his head and ran a thoughtless hand over the three-day stubble on his chin. "She lies ninety percent of the time about where she's going but she always tells us she's going."

"Did anyone mention to her we were leaving early this morning?" Even the colonel had left his desk to see what was happening. "I thought I heard somebody on deck around five- thirty, just after I started work. But I assumed it was Stuart, or Cole, getting things ready for departure."

"Where on earth would she be going at five-thirty in the morning?" Stella wondered out loud.

The question caused a heavy silence to fall over the group until, one by one, all eyes finally settled on Cole. He was leaning against the chart table in the back corner, his troubled face in a turmoil as to whether or not he was going to tell everything he knew. His gaze met Stella's and he took a deep breath. She had been silently willing him to speak up and he read the message as if she said it right to him. However, rather than explain, he simply pulled a folded piece of note paper out of his back pocket and handed it over to Millie.

Dear Family,

I am not fit to be a decent mother or anything else. Please take good care of my boy.

Lou

At which point Millie burst into tears, and the baby right after.

"She's a deuce of a good mother!" Gerald smacked a fist into his palm as if it might somehow help him think. "It's the only thing she is good at!"

"A good mother doesn't desert her own child, no matter what the circumstances," The colonel intoned. And looking up at him from the side, with that rather Grecian profile and wavy silver hair, Stella thought how he resembled one of those ancient prophets whose word was always law. Then, again, he never did have much patience for Lou Edna and all her lies.

"Oh, why do all my children end up leaving me?" Millie choked back a sob to ask. "What's wrong with me? I feel like I'm infected with some kind of curse on families!"

"Millie, that's not true," Stella objected,

bouncing the baby in a soothing motion and trying to comfort her former landlady at the same time. "Why you've got a bigger heart for families than any person I know. Just look at all the people you're family to that aren't even related to you." She didn't mention that she wasn't related to Lou Edna, either, but it didn't seem the time. "Thank you, Stella," Millie sniffed and reached into the pocket of her sweater for a tissue. "It's just you have to wonder when all this love you feel keeps chasing people away."

"We can philosophize, later," said Mason. "Right now, I'm thinking Campbell River is a devil of a big place, and not a one of us here—except Cole—is of an age to be raising another kid. At the very least, we're gonna have to split up just to cover enough ground for a look-see. Then reconnoiter."

Now, Cole straitened to his full height and declared, "I'll find her if I have to—"

"You, mister," said the Captain, in no uncertain terms, "are an illegal alien in this country and will stay aboard ship. Be prepared to fire up the engine in one big hurry, though, in case we have to drag her back kicking and hollering."

"But, Cap, I—"

"No buts. We can't afford the local laws in on this mess. By the hoagie! Do we even have a birth certificate on this kid? They don't take kindly to people dragging other people's kids across borders around here."

A statement which produced another grave silence. "Mason's right," the colonel agreed. "We need a plan." "Well," said the Captain, "seeing how it will be mostly a land maneuver, I'm all for deferring the details to Mase. You're the best expert on how she thinks, anyhow."

"What do I know what she's got in that mixed-up head of hers?" Mason grumbled. "All I know is, if she thinks she can get away with something like this, she's got another thing coming."

By the time the *Dreadnaught* pulled up alongside the courtesy dock in Campbell River, nearly eight hours had gone by since Lou Edna had left the boat. So, it was a sombre group that headed off to scour near-by hotels and cafes where one might while away hours waiting for a flight back to the States. Not being able to catch an immediate flight out was really their only hope, considering the girl always had a stash of emergency funds for a quick escape.

It was a habit left over from living in so many dreadful places before Mason (who had done his banking where Lou worked), noticed she was all alone in the world, facing a terrible situation, and took her home to Millie. The two years she had been with "the family" were the longest she lived anywhere in all of her twenty-three years.

Considering how many boardwalks, malls, and shops were a short walk away from the waterfront, each of the five searchers chose a separate street, and agreed to "reconnoiter" after investigating four blocks. A thorough plan that would have cast a sufficiently wide net throughout the vicinity. Only they didn't need to carry it out. No sooner had they started up the docks to take up their positions, a frantic Lou Edna came flying down the ramp, hollering, "Pop—oh, Pop!" before she flung her arms around Mason's neck and cried, "You came back for me —you came back!"

"What did you expect, girlie? You left something important behind!"

"Cole said he'd be better off without me. And it's true!" She was dressed for obscurity (Stella knew a lot about runaways): jeans, navy-blue sweatshirt with tennis shoes and backpack. Little of her face was visible under a ball-cap and sunglasses. "But I just felt worse the farther I got away from him. Then I couldn't get back fast enough—you already left!"

"Had to leave early to catch the right tides," said Stuart.

"Cole didn't tell us you were gone until he

got off watch at ten!" Millie sniffed as the girl flew into her arms next (like a chick returning to a mother hen). "What a scare you gave us, honey—what were you thinking?"

"I don't know. I was just trying to do right for my boy!"

"Two wrongs don't make a right," Stuart declared, in a tone loud enough to call all hands. "You jumped ship. No crew of mine ever pulled that on me before and I don't take kindly to it."

"Maybe we should talk about this when we get back aboard," said the colonel, noticing several onlookers nearby. "Especially since Gerald might slip into apoplexy the longer we're gone."

The engine roared to life as soon as they approached— evidence that Cole was taking his part in the plan as serious as the rest of them had. Stuart left briefly to untie dock lines and set a course back toward the narrows, where they would pull over into a nearby cove and wait for the tide to turn. Again. Meanwhile, the rest of the group settled around the large wooden dining table in the galley to talk things over.

It had a brass lantern hanging above it that Stella had originally thought was simply for decoration. However, it was a fully operative kerosene lamp that gave off quite the cheery glow when it was lit. Something of a rarity on this trip because it stayed light until nearly bedtime around here. So, at the moment, there was plenty of light filtering in through the several large portholes in various places around the area. Gerald came in to join them, after Lou checked in on the baby, who was taking a late afternoon nap in the miniature swinging hammock his Uncle Gerry had set up for him in his own stateroom. In fact, they all had accommodations for the baby in their rooms since his mother was forever needing someone else to watch him.

"You should have at least talked it over with somebody," he was saying as the two of them returned to the galley. "Got a second opinion and all that. A decision made in haste almost never works out."

"I'll try to remember that next time I feel like jumping ship." Lou Edna sank down onto the edge of one of the upholstered benches and didn't take off her sun glasses, only pulled her ball cap down lower over her eyes. Another warning sign as far as Stella was concerned. People only wore sun glasses inside when they wanted to hide something. More lies, probably. She turned on one of the propane burners on the large iron cook-stove and set a huge stainless steel kettle on to boil. A cup of tea always made times like these go smoother, in her estimation.

"All right, let's have it." Mason removed his fisherman's cap and set it on the back of the seat. "And take those glasses off. I don't like talking to someone I can't see."

"I'd rather not," Lou Edna replied.

"Why in heaven's name?" Millie asked, and then gasped at her own unspoken answer. "Lou, you aren't—you didn't—"

"Girlie, you better not be," Mason interrupted. "We been through that, already, and once was enough."

The girl sighed and rested her head in her hands for a moment. "Sometimes, I just wish I was dead."

"Don't say that!" said Millie, who must have experienced similar thoughts during her own lowest moments and could identify. "Next thing you know, that's all you can think about."

"You've got a boy in the other room whose sun rises and sets on you," the colonel reminded her gently. It was the first time Stella could remember him saying anything encouraging to Lou Edna. "In his eyes, you're perfect."

"It's true," Stella agreed. "The greatest influence on any child is their own parents. It's a proven fact."

"He'll never forgive me," she mourned.

"What's to forgive?" Gerald argued. "He's so little he doesn't know the difference."

"Oh, somebody will tell him, they always do."

"Unless somebody else..." It was Cole's voice instead of Stuart's coming from the doorway as he came through. "Straitens up and makes some changes. So the kid at least has a mother he can look up to."

"Nobody can change what they don't feel, Cole."

"Who needs to feel it? Just find out what's normal and do it." "You should talk. Right?"

"Well, he's right about that, anyway," the colonel pointed out. "Doing right is a precursor to feeling what's right. It's the way one learns to judge between right and wrong. Good and evil, you might say."

"Are you saying I'm evil, now, Mr. Colonel?"

"Don't get sassy, girlie," Mason warned. "And take off those sun glasses. You got people who care enough about you to try and help figure things out—show a little respect."

"I don't feel like it."

In answer, he reached across the table, lightly knocked the bill of her ball cap up and snatched them off. Only to reveal a glaring bruise that circled her left eye and the bridge of her nose. An audible gasp escaped Stella. Millie said, "Oh, no!" And Gerald leaped to his feet so fast he teetered then caught his balance before darting at Cole.

"Hey, wait a minute..." The younger man stood up to his full height and pointed a warning finger at the ridiculous figure coming at him in his half serape hanging over a green sweat suit "You just wait one minute!"

"Put 'em up!" Gerald danced back and forth on his feet in front of him and began to circle his fists. "You woman beater!"

"Don't make me pop you one, old man. You hear me?"

"Nobody's gonna pop anybody," said Mason. "Sit down, Gerry."

About three seconds before Gerald surprised everyone with a lightning-quick punch that knocked Cole DeForio in the nose so hard it started to gush blood, and sent him sprawling backward onto the floor.

5

Somebody hollered and the men got up to intervene. But it was unnecessary. Gerald staggered back at the realization of what he had done and sank down onto the nearest edge of the dining table so he wouldn't slip into a dead faint. Stella hurried to get a cold cloth to stop the bleeding, as everyone else hovered around Cole and tried to get him back on his feet, again. Which wasn't having much effect since he wasn't responding.

"Good grief—" Gerald pulled his watch-cap off and ran a hand through his thinning brown hair. "Isn't dead, is he? Didn't mean to do all that. Oh, I say!"

"He's out cold," Mason pronounced. "Where'd you learn to fight like that, Gerry?"

"Alarming number of people liked to beat up on me, when I was young, so I took boxing lessons. Don't know what came over me to hit him so hard. Must have done it in a blaze of anger."

"I'll say you did," said Lou Edna. "Serves him right!"

"He's coming to," the colonel observed just before the victim moaned and uttered a muffled curse.

Suddenly, there were two bells in rapid succession, then another two, and the young man struggled to get to his feet.

"You better stay put till the bleeding stops," Mason suggested. "It's just Stuart wanting to drop the anchor outside those narrows and wait for the tide to change. And don't anybody go anywhere," he added as he started for the door that led out to the decks. "We're going to get to the bottom of all this, one way or the other. You hear me, Shortcake?"

"Pop, I came back—isn't that enough?"

"No."

"Well, I don't approve of any of it." Millie returned to the table and stirred three spoons of sugar into the tea she had poured from the things Stella set out earlier. "Resorting to physical violence is no way to solve problems."

"I agree," said Stella. "Cole, have you

ever thought of taking a course in anger management?"

"Anger management—tell that to Lou. It was self-defense. She was hammering my gut like she was contending for some heavyweight championship."

"I don't have an ounce of fat on my body! Hit him, again, Gerry."

"E-gads—I'm still shaking from last time. I detest it when things get bloody, I really do."

"Lou Edna Wilson!" Millie set her mug down so hard tea sloshed out. "What on earth has gotten into you?"

"I'm regretting smuggling somebody aboard, that's what's got into me. Been all high and mighty ever since Cap promoted him. Like nobody else is good enough, anymore. I'd have taken the Senator with me if I didn't have to get another job and find a place to live, first. I wasn't really leaving him. I was going to send for him as soon as I got settled."

"And where were your going to send to—general delivery, Alaska? We don't know exactly where the lodge is, we have to find it first. Then maybe it won't even be livable and we'd have to go somewhere else."

"Cap would have told me when he got back."

"Maybe he won't want to go all the way back. He's part of the family, now. But I have to tell you, Lou, it practically killed me you would leave without saying anything. After everything we've been through!"

"I'm not leaving you, Millie, I'm leaving him." She pointed to where Cole was still sitting on the floor with the wet cloth against his face. "What kind of mother would stay with somebody violent? But I knew you all needed him for crew so I didn't think I should say anything."

"Lou, if you tell one more lie, you'll be sorry," Cole mumbled from behind the cloth.

"Truth is the basis of all genuine relationships," the Colonel pointed out. A remark that caused Stella some discomfort because she still hadn't made time for that heart-to-heart she felt she owed him, yet, either. Even though she intended to.

"Keeping plans to yourself is not lying, Cole—I do not lie to this family!"

A statement that brought her young man up off the floor so fast, no one was ready for it. But instead of going after Lou Edna, he snatched the backpack she had set on the upholstered bench beside her, instead.

"Give it back to me!" she hollered. "Don't you dare!"

He dared. Even when she picked up Millie's tea and threw it at him, he only ducked and fended it off before unzipping and dumping the contents out on the table for all to see. Millie screamed. The colonel's eyes widened and his mouth dropped open, while Stella—who had stood up that very moment, in order to step between the two before they resorted to an out-and- out brawl—was just in time to catch Gerald before he fell off the table, onto the floor.

There was an assortment of credit cards belonging to various family members in the heap, the colonel's gold pocket- watch the military academy had given him when he retired, and several of Stella's autographed first editions from her book shelves. There was also a genuine shrunken head Gerald had paid a lot of money for on an archaeological dig in the South Pacific before his invalid days. But the things that had elicited a scream from Millie, and got her reaching for her heart pills, was the notorious *Villa Nofre* jewelry collection that belonged to the owner's last wife and had been missing for years.

"Where did you get those!" the mansion's

former landlady could barely manage a frightened whisper.

"In a trunk up in the attic," Lou Edna admitted. "When I was looking for things to pawn that you wouldn't notice. Now, you'll probably never trust me again. None of you will!" At which point she buried her face in her arms on the table and gave way to more tears.

"E-gads—those things are worth a fortune—we could all go to jail for this. We're accomplices! What are we going to do, Mil? E.J.'s been a good sport but I doubt he'd let us off three times. First the household valuables, then the paintings, and now the missing jewels! He'd never believe us a third time!"

"Oh, I don't know what to do—Mason's going to hit the roof when he hears this! You couldn't have got away with pawning those, Lou. The family lawyers have had detectives and everyone else trying to find them for years. The lady who owned them was a Russian refugee who came over here after World War II—some distant cousin to a Czar, or something."

"They're extremely well-documented," added Gerald, then grimaced at the very thought.

"We seem to be going from the frying pan

into the fire every time we turn around, lately," said the colonel. "The amount of trouble this incident could have caused every one of us."

"Don't you have any feelings at all for us, Lou?" Millie implored. "We've shared everything we had with you, and you do something like this!"

"I didn't know they were that valuable—I didn't!"

"You definitely knew the value of everything else," said the colonel. "And a good idea of how to liquidate them, seeing how fast you were headed back home."

"What did you take us for?" Gerald pulled a handkerchief out of his pocket and dabbed at the beads of sweat gathering on his forehead. "A bunch of pushovers?"

"I'm afraid, that's exactly what she took us for," the colonel replied for her. "Except considering what terrible things might backfire in your own life as a result of this act, makes you something of a pushover, yourself, Lou Edna."

"Now, what am I going to do?" she wailed. "If my boy ends up in foster care, I'll kill myself!"

"That wouldn't help one bit," said Stella.

"I am a horrible person—just like Cole

said! There's no hope for me!"

"Of course there's hope for you," said the colonel. "There's hope for everyone who truly wants it. You only have to ask." "Nobody will ever forgive me for this—oh, I could just die!"

"There is one person who will," he replied. "And he already did the dying."

"What good would it be if I end up all alone? None of you will want me around anymore!"

"Young lady, you would never be alone in this world, again.

That, I can promise you. With only a few words from you, right here and now, your entire life can be turned around. But it has to be genuine. You'd be talking to the one who knows every thought and intent of your heart, yet still loves you enough to give you a second chance. So... what do you say?"

"Stella," the colonel said later that evening, without looking up from his laptop. "You haven't read a word since you opened that book. Is there something bothering you? Something you'd like to talk about?"

"I just can't get over how Lou Edna responded to you. I even think that was a genuine prayer of forgiveness she prayed. Right in front of all of us."

"Well, it wasn't me she was responding to. I was just the messenger."

"But how did you know she was ready to pray? She jumped at your suggestion so fast, I think she was actually waiting to." "I didn't know. But since she might never have a remorseful moment like that, again, I thought I better press the issue. Seems to have worked out."

"It certainly did. Why the change that

came over her was practically instant. It was like you could almost see some great weight lifted off her. And it was so touching how Cole came over and hugged her so tenderly afterward. He must have a good heart, himself, to want so much for her to do things right. Maybe he was touched by the love of God at sometime in his life, too."

He smiled, then gave half a chuckle at the memory. "That's what really changes people, you know. The love of God. It's super-natural."

"Oh, it is!" she agreed. "In a good way."

"I'd say the love of God can't be anything but good."

"I was talking about the supernatural part. There are some supernatural things that aren't good at all. Wouldn't you agree?" "Most definitely. But you wouldn't want anything to do with that sort of stuff, would you? Life is too short to fit everything in the world into it. And—as long as we get to choose—wouldn't you rather fill yours up with good things?"

"Of course I would. But sometimes we don't have any say in the matter."

"We always have some kind of choice, Stel. Sometimes it's only a very small one. But if you look close enough, you'll find it's a way out. Had that happen to me, personally, many times."

Stella thought how looking for a way out is what brought on the worst trouble in her life. But she certainly didn't want to get into that subject at the moment. The troubles at hand were more than enough to deal with. "I wish I could be that sure. I mean, it must be very comforting to have so much assurance."

"Well, I didn't get it all at once, you know. Just little by little, one choice at a time. Small adjustments, you might say. Life's full of choices—there are dozens every day. How's the saying go..." He cocked his head and thought for a moment. "I have set before you life and death—oh, that you would choose life! The more you practice choosing life, the better you get at it. Sort of a win-win situation."

"I hope Lou Edna discovers that. If she could only know that choosing to do wrong is what actually diminishes her opportunities. Not life being harder on her than anyone else. She's a smart girl, though. So, maybe it won't take too long for her to realize she can get better options to choose from each time she makes a good choice."

"Well spoken. And that's exactly what she would hear if she got some good counseling to overcome some of her past perceptions."

Stella thought how that was exactly where she had heard it but she didn't say anything about that, either.

"However—now that she's asked for it—she'll get plenty of supernatural help to make sure she succeeds," he went on, "as do we all. None of us are much of a match for the dark side of those spiritual realms. Some of us are just more susceptible to it than others. More easily taken in, you might say. Especially considering those dark forces have the ability to masquerade as creatures of light, for a time."

A thought that gave Stella something of a jolt—how in the world could a person tell the difference?

"The danger," the colonel went on, "is that their purpose is to trap you, not give you a way out of anything. They can only lead a person to death and destruction. No mortal is a match for that. Never has been. Which I suppose is why we get so tossed around between good and evil in the first place."

There was the opening. Stella realized, right then, that she needed to know how one went about getting that good kind of supernatural help, in order to escape the bad. Because it suddenly became very clear that she had allowed frightening things to rule her life, too. So, she closed her book, took a deep breath, and jumped in.

"You know something, Oliver? I think I've been one of the deceived ones. Before I got my new life, I was convinced the only future I had was to end up in a good rest home instead of a bad one. I guess you could say I was a pushover for the darker side of supernatural, too."

"And look at you, now, Stel. Doing wonderful things a lot of younger people don't even get to do. You're on the adventure of a lifetime!"

"Makes me not want to ever look at the dark side of supernatural, again."

"And rightfully so. It's like opening up a can of worms. Nothing good can ever come of it. Just has some sort of curious appeal. Especially to people who are searching for something more than just everyday living. Which we all do at some point in our lives."

"That's sort of what I meant by not always having a choice with those types of encounters. Every once in a while something just... pops up in front of you and you bump into it. What I'm trying to say is... do you believe in ghosts, Oliver? Tortured souls that roam the earth for some horrid reason, or other?"

"I believe they aren't always tortured souls."

"What are they, then?"

He looked at her for a few moments, then closed his laptop and came over to join her on the couch. "Oh, I don't think it matters much, really. I only know there is no form of darkness that doesn't run for the shadows as soon as a light comes on. Which is why I make such a point of standing as close to the one who created light as I possibly can. That way, I'm not so apt to trip over things. None of us can see in the dark, anyway."

"I've certainly never thought of it like that before. But it does make more sense to look at it that way, now that you mention it. Especially since Gerald told me he's had more trouble since he started delving into those things than he ever had before that. Did you know he actually used to try to encounter ghosts? He studied old legends and went looking for them. Was even thinking of doing his master's on some ghost over in England. But he says he's never been the same since. Seems to be plagued with them everywhere he goes, now."

"My point exactly. If you ask me, it's half

what's deteriorating his health."

"That's exactly what he said."

"Yes, and he's always after some new incantation to ward them off, too. You know he sleeps with tin foil over his head? That's why he wears a watch-cap to bed. To keep it in place."

"He's talked to you about it before?"

"Oh, we've had any number of talks about it. I advised it would be better to say a quick prayer and tell them to buzz off." "You know, that's just what he did last night when I ran into him in the companionway. He called me a—a foul spirit—and told me to get away. Thought I was another one of his apparitions. That's what he calls them. Apparitions."

"I'd say that wasn't far wrong." Then he laughed trying to imagine the scene. "Just goes to show you never know when someone is really listening to you."

"Oliver?"

"Yes, my dear?"

"I've been seeing some sort of..." She smoothed a wrinkle out of the rose-colored throw she had over her lap. "Apparition, myself. A very distinct one, in fact."

"Well, the next time you do, say a prayer, and tell it to buzz off. Better yet—wake me up, Stel—and we'll face the thing down together!"

"Really?"

"Absolutely. 'If one can put a thousand to flight, two can put ten-thousand to flight,' as the scripture says."

"It does?"

"Yes. You can always bank on the scriptures. They're truth in its purest form."

"Well, Oliver, I..." Stella looked at the man she had married barely a month ago, and suddenly felt as if she had found a rare treasure. And he wasn't even irritated with her! Now, the thought that he cared enough to walk with her even through the dark places gave her the most wonderful sense of well-being she had ever known. "Oliver Henry?" She slid closer and nestled into that comfortable, always ready, embrace that she loved so much. "I think you're the most amazing man I've ever known!"

"Believe me, I could say the same thing about you, dearest."

"Me? I don't think I've done much of anything amazing in my entire life."

"Oh, I don't know. I'll never forget the way you looked catching old Gerry before he fell on the floor. You're always the first to jump right in whenever something goes wrong. Remember when you wanted me to sign that petition to save good literature?"

"I remember I interrupted you when you were working on your hero book. But I didn't know that back then."

"Ah, I needed a good interruption right about then. I was getting too stuffy. You know, it takes an amazing woman to bring out the best in a man. That's what you've done for me." Then he gave her an affectionate squeeze. "What a match we are, Stella Madison Henry—I have a feeling we're going to make a great team!"

Author's Note

Every once in a while, someone comes along who can see the world through eyes of great understanding. If that person is also a good communicator they can help many people during their lives. But if that person also happens to be an artist, the world may keep their treasures throughout generations. Art— whether music, painting, literature, or drama—touches the heart faster than anything else. Especially if it's beautiful. And most especially if it mirrors some universal feeling that resides within the heart of all humanity.

Such was the case with Alfred Tennyson, who is one of the nine most quoted writers in the *Oxford Dictionary of Quotations*. A poet who ultimately became appointed by royal decree as the Poet Laureate of England and Ireland, he possessed the rare talent of not only being able express the deeper feelings of human experience but to express them in a way people did not want to ever forget.

As the son of a pastor, and raised in a moral home, he was blessed with a wonderful sensitivity and compassion for others. Being able to write about these feelings so beautifully became a mirror of common emotion that resonated throughout the world, even during his own lifetime. A good example is the quote at the beginning of this story which states in so few words, one of the deepest perplexities of life that we all eventually grapple with.

While it is human nature to seek after truth, it is also one of our strongest impulses to try and separate ourselves from things that are false. So, anything that helps enlighten which-is-which for us, is a real gem. Such wisdom distilled down to its purest thoughts can be a great comfort during times of deepest stress, or sorrow.

In seeking out an appropriate quote for the subject of *The Pushover Plot*, I discovered that Alfred Tennyson was the author of many other wonderful quotes I had written into my notebooks over the years. So, the research for this little bit of truth I like to tack onto the end of each story, was more like a surprise visit from an old friend.

Maybe you will find that true, as well.

You can read more of Alfred Tennyson's work, for free, at many places online.

About Lilly Maytree

Lilly Maytree is the author of *Gold Trap, The Pandora Box,* and *The Stella Madison Capers.* Books that sent her careening along on her "Mystery Tours" with her captain husband aboard the *Glory B.* She loves sharing these adventures with readers. It has even been said that she time-travels (but that's probably just a rumor). To find out about her current adventures, simply visit:

www.LillyMaytree.com

Other Books by

Lilly Maytree

Novels...

Gold Trap

Megan Jennings is headed to Africa for high adventure and divine appointments until she makes a small wrong turn. But what is faith, if not to strike out against impossible odds believing you will win? Or leap out into the dark knowing someone will be there to catch you? Someone does catch her... but it isn't who she was expecting.

The Pandora Box

Journalist D.J. Parker learns the location of a famous cache of diamonds that were stolen during World War II. What she doesn't know is— the federal government has been following the case for years. With an old journal to lead the way, she sets out aboard a yacht that once carried the infamous Herman Goering. A thrilling treasure hunt that could either prove to be the adventure of a lifetime... or her worst nightmare.

Home Before Dark
(Caper #1)

Here is the first of the Stella Madison Capers, the story of how everything started, and how she escaped from a catastrophe that seemed to come out of nowhere. Which is the nature of catastrophes but it's so hard to be logical when you're in the middle of one. It's also the story of how she met the colonel (if you're interested in that sort of thing).

A Thief in the House
(Caper #2)

Stella Madison is back, this time with a bevy of friends. But just how far should a person go when it comes to sticking by their friends? There's a thief in the rambling old mansion she moved into. And while it was someone who was quick to lend help when Stella needed it most, how can she possibly return the favor without jeopardizing herself along with them? No person is obligated to go that far... right?

Voyage of the Dreadnaught
collection of four Stella Madison Capers

Here is a collection of the four Stella Madison Capers covering the entire voyage of the *Dreadnaught*, through the Inside Passage to Alaska. Includes: *Sea Trials, The Pushover Plot, Lost in the Wilderness*, and *The Last Resort*. Also includes a brief account of Lilly Maytree's true-life voyage along the same route, in the sailboat *Glory B.*

For Writers...
Unspoken Rules

Popular books (those stories everyone likes no matter what the subject) all have certain things in common. And what they have most in common is what they DON'T do. Within the following pages, dear writer, you will find the three most important "don'ts" of popular fiction that I learned when I was studying the masters. Why? Because I love research and I never mind sharing my notes.

Writing Rules!
(a mysterious student handbook)

A mysterious little desktop handbook that can help anyone (well, almost anyone) with writing rules. Especially if you are a student and have to write things all the time.

For Parents...

Behave Yourself!
Teaching your children to discipline themselves.

Are you tired of bickering during daily routines encroaching on way too much of your family time? Here is a book that offers a two-week program that teaches your children to discipline themselves. Hard to believe? Here are the step-by-step secrets of how it's done, and why it works.

The Nature of Children
(And how to deal with it.)

A manual based on a compilation of

parenting articles Lilly wrote over several years as a columnist for Childcare Magazine. It is a result of many requests from parents for more information about that content and the foundation of the methods she used both in raising her own children, and in her classrooms.

After years of experience, she has a lot to say about what motivates children and has implemented many of her unique ideas into books and programs that others can use.

For autographed copies, visit:

www.LillyMaytree.com

*"I have never been lost, but I will admit to
being confused for several weeks."*

Daniel Boone

1

Stella Madison opened the door to the after-deck and a blast of cold wind hit her face. Why did Millie want to meet out here? The galley of the *Dreadnaught* was so much more comfortable and cozy. Of course there was always someone else passing through it.

"I brought us some tea, Millie." She set the tray down on a small table between two deck lounges.

"Oh, thanks, Stel." Her former landlady set her knitting aside and tightened the black-and-white checkered scarf under her chin that she had wrapped around her auburn hair." Something hot would be good about now."

"It's awfully cold out here." Stella pulled

her periwinkle blue knit cap down lower over her fluffy white hair that was just long enough to tuck under. and zipped her jacket all the way up.

"We're in Alaska, now. Mason says we have been ever since we crossed that Dixon Entrance, with all those fishing boats we had to dodge in and out of. Said if we didn't have to go all the way to Ketchikan to get back through customs again, we could be almost to the lodge by now. Mmm... Orange Spice. My favorite."

"Mine's the Moroccan Mint. Except Orange Spice just seemed warmer this morning." She sat down in the other lounge chair and unfolded a green wool blanket over her lap."Captain Stuart sure brought home a lot of souvenirs from his Navy days. Every chair on this boat has one of these. Thank goodness."

"They're Army-issue. I think half the things aboard he got from one of those old Army surplus places back home." "Well, looks aren't everything. They're nice and warm, anyway. Imagine being almost to the lodge, Millie. I can hardly wait to see it."

"Me, too. It will definitely be a load off my mind to get on solid ground, again."

"I thought you liked living on the boat."

"I do. It's got all kinds of ambiance. And that galley is heaven to cook in. It's the ocean I'm scared stiff of. Don't think I ever will get used to it." She set her cup down and picked up her knitting, again.

Stella was about to take another sip of her tea when she realized her friend's project was a sock with such an enormous tube it would go way past a person's knee, already. "Millie, who on earth is that for?"

"This? Oh, it isn't for anybody. I just knit to settle my nerves. The only thing I ever learned to do was socks. Way back when I was ten. Took me half the trip even to remember how to do it because it's been that long since I practiced." As if to prove the point, she began to unravel it, again.

Stella gasped at seeing the thing disappear into a heap of wrinkly gray yarn right before her eyes. "But all that work— wouldn't you rather have something to show for it? Give them away for Christmas, maybe."

"They're not good enough for that. They always turn out crooked or something. But a person has to resort to some form of therapy when they're scared half out of their mind most of the time. Wouldn't you say?"

"I guess it depends on what you're scared of. The colonel says if it's something evil, you just tell it to buzz off, because you don't want anything to do with the dark side of supernatural. But if it's something legitimate like the ocean, I don't blame you. I was scared stiff myself during that storm we had. And I don't like it when it gets rough and choppy, either. But it must at least make you feel better that we're almost there."

"The truth is, Stel, I'm even more scared about getting there. Because of the bears. Mason says just make a lot of noise and stay in groups. On account of they don't want anything to do with us, either."

"Well, that sounds reasonable, don't you think?"

"Not as reasonable as having a loaded gun on my belt." Stella wasn't sure if she would be more afraid of Millie walking around with a loaded gun than a bear but she didn't mention it.

"Bears you can shoot. But the ocean..." She got to the end of unraveling her sock and started casting on new stitches, again. "The ocean is so unpredictable and... big. I really don't know how Stuart even finds his way around in it. Especially without radar."

"We don't have radar?"

"Too expensive, and he never had the funds."

"For heaven sake, I didn't know that." She felt a twinge of apprehension at the very thought. "He's so confident about everything, I just assumed."

"Used to be confident. Which is really why I asked you to come out here, Stel." Millie stopped working, and looked her right in the eye. "Something is wrong with Stuart. He hasn't been himself the last couple of weeks."

"Well, he does have a lot more to worry about than the rest of us. The Dreadful being his boat, and all."

"It's the *Dreadnaught,* not the Dreadful. Sometimes I think you enjoy calling it that."

"I do. It's such a monstrosity of a thing. Although I have to admit it has its charm. I'll probably be won over by the time we finally get there." She took another sip of her tea and noticed Millie had dropped two stitches by the time she went back to her knitting. "But Captain Stuart has such peculiar ways, I don't see how you can tell if he's his normal self or not. He's one of the most abnormal people I've ever known."

"I can tell, all right. He only ate half his linguine and clams the other night and that's one of his favorite meals. He never used to miss when I made it back home."

"Maybe he's just not used to all our home-cooked meals. Didn't Mason say he lived mostly off boiled eggs, crackers, and sardines?"

"That and junk food. Which is why I decided to make hamburgers and fries for our celebration, tonight. That's his other favorite. The rest of of us won't mind as long as we barbecue and fill things out with your New England baked beans and Lou's fruit salad. If he doesn't eat any of that, we'll know something's definitely wrong. You think?"

"I'm thinking what would we do if anything happened to Captain Stuart. Maybe the rest of us should try to carry more of the load for a while. Could be he's coming down with something and just needs a rest."

"Could be. But I'm going to keep my eye on him during our Alaska celebration. Then slip him a good physic if I think he isn't quite right."

"Why, Millie—that's an awful thing to do to somebody. You should ask, first."

"He wouldn't take it at all, if I asked. Better just to slip it into his tea."

End of Excerpt

To read the rest of this Stella Madison Caper, visit us online at:

LightsmithPublishers.com

Also available from Ingram wherever books are sold.

If you enjoyed reading this
"Little Traveling Book"
please share it with someone!

If you have children (or know any), you
may even enjoy browsing the *"mysteriously
different books"* over at:

SummersIslandPress.com

9 781944 798475